IN THEIR OWN WORDS

TITANIC

A Primary Source History

Senan Molony

GARETH**STEVENS**

GS

PUBLISHING

A Member of the WRC Media Family of Companies

KEY TO SYMBOLS
The following symbols highlight the sources of material from the past.

FILM EXCERPT
Primary source material from a movie about the subject matter.

SONG EXCERPT
Text from songs or poems about the subject matter.

OFFICIAL SPEECH
Transcribed words from official government speeches.

GOVERNMENT DOCUMENT
Text from an official government document.

LETTER
Text from a letter written by a participant in the events.

PLAQUE/INSCRIPTION
Text from plaques or monuments erected in memory of events in this book.

INTERVIEW/BOOK EXTRACT
Text from an interview or book.

NEWSPAPER ARTICLE
Extracts from newspapers of the period.

TELEGRAM
Text from a telegram sent to or by a participant in the events.

Cover Photos:
Top: Titanic's *Captain Edward John Smith, who planned to retire after the crossing, went down with the ship.*
Bottom: *The Titanic's bow lies rusting about 2.5 miles (4 kilometers) below the surface of the Atlantic Ocean.*

CONTENTS

Above: *The Titanic traveled from Southampton, England, to Cherbourg, France, and then to Queenstown (now Cobh), Ireland, before starting across the Atlantic. It never reached New York, its final destination. It sank 1,000 miles (1,600 km) due east of Boston, Massachusetts, and 350 miles (560 km) southeast of Cape Race in Newfoundland, Canada.*

Below: *The Titanic's owners, the White Star Line, launched lavish brochures to promote its superliners.*

*W*hen the Titanic *set sail on its maiden voyage in 1912, this true giant of a ship was the pride of Great Britain. It was the most luxurious liner in the world and was said to be the safest vessel ever built. But when it blundered into an iceberg in the near mid-Atlantic, the* Titanic *become the most famous shipwreck in history. It was almost impossible to imagine that one of the largest ships ever built could fail to reach its destination, yet far out to sea, with the nearest point of land 350 miles (560 kilometers) away, the* Titanic *sank beneath the waves. More than 1,500 passengers lost their lives.*

In 1907, officials at the White Star Line shipping company decided to build the world's finest superships—bigger, safer, and more luxurious than any other ships on the water. The first of these ships, the *Olympic,* was launched in 1911 and was followed by its sister ship the *Titanic* just a year later. The two ships were the biggest moving objects ever built, and an article written as the *Titanic* was being constructed claimed it was "practically unsinkable." Yet when it hit an iceberg on the night of April 14, 1912, it did sink. Only 711 people escaped the sinking ship—fewer than a third of those aboard.

In some ways the ship was just unfortunate. The iceberg that sank the 882-foot (269-meter) superliner was not white, like most bergs, but black because it had recently capsized. The *Titanic* was also traveling at its fastest speed when it sailed into danger. Other contributing factors, however, might have been avoided. Some people believe the captain should have slowed the ship after receiving ice warnings. The *Titanic* also had lifeboat spaces for just 1,200 people, although it was carrying 2,201 passengers and crew. And, despite the relatively long time it took for the ship to sink, nearly 500 lifeboat places were not filled.

After the sinking, official inquiries set up on both sides of the Atlantic attempted to find a reason for the tragedy. Although the captain of the *Titanic* and half its officers died in the sinking, the public still wanted someone to be held accountable. Many people blamed the disaster on reckless navigation, while others pointed to the woeful lack of lifeboats. The official inquiries absolved most of the crew from responsibility, but they also came to many wrong conclusions that were believed for years afterwards. People believed, for example, that the ship did not break in two when it sank, despite the testimony of witnesses who said it did. This belief was accepted as fact until the discovery of the ship's wreckage in 1985 proved otherwise. The inquiries

Center: *A life preserver from the Titanic. The inscription signifies that the ship was registered in the port of Liverpool.*

Below: *A ticket to see the launch of the Titanic in Belfast, Ireland (now Northern Ireland). The launch attracted thousands of spectators.*

Launch
OF
White Star Royal Mail Triple-Screw Steamer
"TITANIC"
At BELFAST,
Wednesday, 31st May, 1911, at 12-15 p.m.
Admit Bearer.

Above: *Postcards marking the launch of the amazing steamer were extremely popular. This one was sent from Great Britain to Germany.*

Below: *A model of the Titanic showing how the ship looks now. Recent engineering evidence suggests that the unsinkable ship experienced a hull failure at the surface and broke into two pieces before it went down.*

did, however, lead to some valuable changes in maritime law. A host of safety reforms were made and are still in place today, including the provision of lifeboats for every person on board a ship. A new body, the International Ice Patrol, was set up to monitor ice conditions in Atlantic and avert similar disasters.

Almost from the moment the *Titanic* sank beneath the icy water, efforts were made to locate the wreck. Some of the search schemes were bizarre, including a plan to locate the boat using electromagnets. The site of the *Titanic* remained elusive, and it was not until the development of electronic detection equipment in the 1980s that the search was successful. The remains of the liner were finally discovered by Dr. Robert Ballard and Jean-Louis Michel on September 1, 1985. Since then, a company that was awarded salvor-in-possession rights, RMS Titanic, Inc., has conducted seven research and recovery expeditions to the wreck site. It has recovered more than 5,500 objects, ranging from personal possessions to a large part of the ship's mighty steel hull. Today, scientists are presented with a huge problem over what to do with the ship's wreckage. Some people are calling for the *Titanic* to be raised from the ocean, conscious of the fact that the ship is decaying rapidly and is likely to break up completely in the near future. Others, however, feel that moving the wreckage would be inappropriate; it is essentially a mass grave, and they believe the remains should be left alone. What seems certain is that the public will continue to be fascinated by the tragic story of this great ship, a story that has been immortalized in music, books, and even a blockbuster movie.

1. NEVER AN ABSOLUTION 2. DISTANT MEMORIES 3. SOUTHAMPTON 4. ROSE
5. LEAVING PORT 6. "TAKE HER TO SEA, MR. MURDOCH" 7. "HARD TO STARBOARD"
8. UNABLE TO STAY, UNWILLING TO LEAVE 9. THE SINKING 10. DEATH OF TITANIC
11. A PROMISE KEPT 12. A LIFE SO CHANGED 13. AN OCEAN OF MEMORIES
14. MY HEART WILL GO ON (LOVE THEME FROM 'TITANIC') PERFORMED BY CELINE DION
15. HYMN TO THE SEA

ALBUM PRODUCED BY JAMES HORNER

Above: Titanic *merchandise, including spin-offs from the 1997 film* Titanic, *is sold all over the world.*

Left: *Kate Winslet and Leonardo DiCaprio played the fictional sweethearts Jack and Rose in the movie* Titanic *(1997). The movie brought in $1 billion at box offices worldwide.*

Above: *A first-class passenger ticket for the Titanic's maiden cruise.*

Above: *Postcard of the Olympic at New York after a collision with a British warship, the HMS Hawke, in September 1911.*

T he Royal Mail Steamer (RMS) Titanic *was the second of a trio of gigantic liners commissioned by the White Star Line, one of the foremost steamship companies of the early twentieth century. The three ships were intended to give White Star Line control of the transatlantic market, taking people from Great Britain and Europe to the United States. They would be magnificent, of unparalleled size, and the last word in luxury.*

TITANIC'S OWNERS

The White Star Line began in 1845 as a company operating emigrant vessels during the Australian gold rush. When the gold rush slowed, the company ran into financial difficulties. In 1868, Thomas Henry Ismay bought the company, and under his new ownership, the White Star Line commissioned ships from the Belfast shipbuilders Harland and Wolff. In 1870, the first ship, the *Oceanic*, was built. It was the world's first superliner and was followed by three sister ships of similar size. In 1891, Thomas Ismay's son, J. (Joseph) Bruce Ismay, was appointed president of the White Star Line, and the company decided to focus exclusively on luxury liners. In 1902, the firm was bought by a U.S. company, the International Mercantile Marine, and two years later, J. Bruce Ismay became president of the company. In 1907, Ismay put forward plans to build two great luxury liners on a scale never seen before, with a third to follow if the first two proved successful. In the ships' plans, the emphasis was on luxury rather than speed, since the Belfast shipyard did not have the technology to compete with White Star Line's rival, Cunard, and their fast ships, *Lusitania* and *Mauretania*. White Star Line's first two "floating hotels" were to be called the *Olympic* and the *Titanic*. A giant gantry—the world's largest—was constructed in Belfast for use in building the two vessels, each weighing 45,000 tons (40,900 metric tonnes).

CLASS SYSTEM

Three million rivets were used to hold together thousands of inch-thick steel plates that made up the *Titanic's* hull—but it was the ship's interior, rather than its impressive hull, that concerned most paying customers. The White Star Line, like

BRILLIANT SCENE at QUEEN'S ISLAND

"The vessel launched yesterday from the yard of Harland and Wolff deserves well her name *Titanic*, for none other would more aptly apply. The day was observed as a holiday by all who could leave work, some of these people joining the many of the leisured class who travelled long distances in order to witness the launch. . . . On the river were many craft from small to large, and these were full to overflowing with sightseers. Five minutes before the appointed time there boomed out a double rocket, that being the signal that all was clear. Once more the whistle rang out, then the signal rockets boomed, the mountain of metal commenced to move, and there burst forth from the throats of the thousands of men, women, and children that were assembled at the yard, from those that filled the boats on the river, and from the great human belt that fringed the opposite shore, a cheer that seemed like tumult—it was a wild roar."

From the *Cork Examiner*, June 1, 1911.

Above: *A White Star Line postcard of Olympic, the Titanic's sister ship.*

July 1908
White Star Line commissions construction of three new superliners.

March 31, 1909
The keel is laid for ship number 401, the *Titanic*.

October 20, 1910
The first of the ships, the *Olympic*, is launched.

May 31, 1911
At 12:15 P.M., the *Titanic* enters water for the first time.

June 1911—March 1912
Hull fitted out. Masts, funnels, and superstructure added.

October 1911
Titanic maiden voyage announced for April 1912.

other lines, divided its vessels into three classes, reflecting the class divisions of society at the time. The cost of tickets varied widely between classes. A one-way ticket in a first-class suite could cost as much as £870 ($4,350), or $50,000 at today's prices; a second-class ticket was £12 ($60); and a third–class ticket was just £7 ($40). The first and second classes were known as "saloon" passengers, while third class became known as "steerage"—perhaps because those who traveled in this class were occupying spaces used by steer, or cattle, on other crossings. Despite the name, third class on the *Titanic* was said to be the equivalent of first class on some other lines. The *Titanic's* higher classes stayed in the upper part of the ship and enjoyed more luxurious surroundings.

LIFE ON BOARD

Early claims about the *Titanic*, perhaps in part encouraged by the owners, suggested that it had a

Below: *The Titanic on the stocks at the Harland and Wolff shipyard in Belfast, Ireland (now Northern Ireland).*

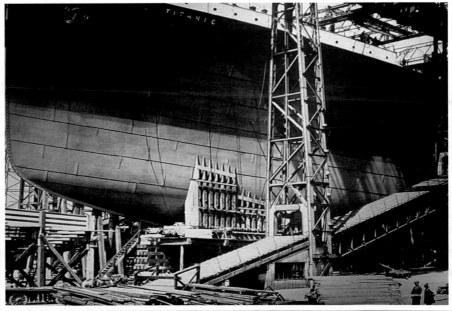

ballroom, a miniature golf course, a skating rink, and even a theater. None of these existed, but it did have a swimming pool, filled with tepid seawater; a gymnasium; a squash court; smoking rooms and bars; libraries; a barbershop; and a verandah café and various other dining facilities. Its passenger accommodations ranged from dormitories in third class to self-contained apartments in first class. Apartments included bedrooms, parlors, private baths, and even a private library. Advance publicity about the *Titanic* pointed out that the ship was "as complete in her safety devices as in her luxurious outfit." The ship was divided into thirty compartments, separated by heavy bulkheads, or steel walls. Supposedly, several of these compartments could flood without compromising safety, but there is no record that the White Star Line ever claimed the ship was "unsinkable."

FOOD ON THE *TITANIC*

Luxuries on the *Titanic* did not end with the accommodations. Menus across all three passenger classes offered a great variety of options. Four meals a day were typical, even in third class. In the opulent surroundings of the first-class dining

Left: *A bronze cherub from the first-class staircase at the stern of the ship.*

Below: *One of the grand staircases on board the* Titanic.

Above: *An artist's impression of a second-class bedroom on the* Titanic.

March 25, 1912
Recruits sign up to crew *Titanic*. Men hired in Southampton will be sent to Belfast for the launch.

March 27, 1912
Captain Herbert Haddock in temporary charge. He will be replaced by Edward Smith.

April 1, 1912
High winds cause sea trials to be postponed.

April 2, 1912
Trials successful. Ship accepted by White Star. *Titanic* departs Belfast at night for Southampton.

April 3, 1912
Spontaneous fire smolders in a coal bunker close to the bows. Minor stokehold flood.

April 4, 1912
Titanic berths at Ocean Dock in Southampton.

room, passengers could enjoy an eleven-course meal each night. A typical meal might start with oysters, washed down with a fine white Burgundy wine. A soup course came next, followed by a fish dish, a main course of beef or chicken, then a second main course which could be lamb with mint sauce, roast duckling with apple sauce, or beef sirloin. Punch or sorbet came next to cleanse the palate, followed by the small seventh, eighth, and ninth courses of delicacies such as roast squab, cold asparagus, and pâté de foie gras— pureed goose liver. Choices for the tenth course, dessert, included Waldorf pudding, chocolate and vanilla éclairs, French ice cream, and peaches in jelly. The eleventh course was an assortment of fresh fruits and mature cheese. Dinner then concluded with tea or coffee, and waiters came around to offer the gentlemen their choice of cigar. A different menu was offered each night.

The *Titanic*'s provisions included 45,000 napkins, 50,000 towels, 18,000 sheets, 7,500 blankets, 5,000 table cloths, 800 eiderdown quilts, 12,000 knives, 12,000 forks, 19,000 spoons, 400 sugar basins, 400 cream jugs, 1,000 finger bowls, 12,000 cups and saucers, 1,200 teapots, and 2,500 champagne glasses.

"The provisioning for one voyage alone tots up to such an onerous sum that few people would credit the figure if published, so that people are better left to their imaginations as to what it would cost to provide for three classes of travellers numbering in all about 3,100 souls, over an ocean journey of less than seven days out and the same time home, and provision for a crew of about 800 for one week in America."

From the *Southampton Pictorial*, March 18, 1912.

Above: *King Edward VII was on the British throne when the* Titanic *was built and launched. At that time, Great Britain was an industrial powerhouse and had world-class shipbuilders.*

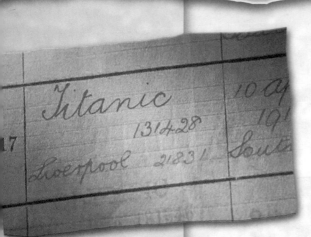

The Titanic *had a largely trouble-free delivery journey from Belfast, Ireland, where it was built, to Southampton, England, the starting point of its maiden voyage to New York. Two incidents—a small fire and water entering a boiler room through a blocked pump—were not considered serious by the ship's crew. When it arrived, the* Titanic *had only a skeleton crew aboard and one paying passenger from Belfast. The bulk of the crew would be taken on in Southampton.*

Above: *A fragment from a notebook indicating the amount of coal to be taken on board the Titanic.*

Below: *A lifeboat nameplate from the Titanic, removed by a carpenter on the ship that was later to come to the ship's rescue.*

SAILING DAY

The *Titanic* spent a week in Southampton while the crew prepared it for its journey to New York. More than 6,000 tons (6,600 m tonnes) of coal for fuel had to be collected from nearby ships because a national miner's strike had affected supplies. The ship was scrubbed throughout, and its 70-foot (21-m) funnels (smokestacks) were cleaned.

All cargo was brought on board. The number of crew on board reached more than 890, but one officer was reassigned elsewhere. This officer, David Blair, took with him a pair of binoculars he had been lending to the lookouts. These binoculars were never replaced. The *Titanic* was ready to set sail on Wednesday, April 10, 1912. By mid-morning, passengers had begun to board the ship. The British Board of Trade completed pre-voyage checks to ensure that the *Titanic* complied with safety and hygiene regulations. These checks included the lowering of two lifeboats, mainly to see that they were seaworthy. The boats were swiftly hauled back aboard and made secure. The *Titanic* also was required by company regulations to hold a lifeboat drill on the voyage to familiarize the crew with lifeboat stations. It was not, however, a legal

Fireman Joe Mulholland said that Thomas Andrews, the representative of shipbuilders Harland & Wolff, came down to the stokehold on the *Titanic's* trip from Belfast to Southampton. He pointed to "insulting slogans about the Pope," which had been chalked up on the smoke-box. . . . "He said: 'They are disgusting' and went off and returned with some sailors and had them removed."

Mulholland recalled that before the *Titanic* set sail from Belfast, he took pity on a stray cat that was about to have kittens and brought it aboard. At Southampton he was wondering whether to stay on board or leave the ship and take a job as storekeeper, when another seaman called him over and said: "Look Big Joe. There's your cat taking its kittens down the gang-plank." "That settled it. I went and got my bag and that's the last I saw of the *Titanic*."

From the *Sunday Independent*, April 15, 1962.

8 A.M.
First of the "transatlantic" trains leaves Waterloo for Southampton.

9:30 A.M.
J. Bruce Ismay, managing director of the White Star Line, inspects *Titanic* with his wife and young children. He will remain aboard alone for the crossing.

12:15 P.M.
Titanic whistle blown three times to signal departure.

12:20 P.M.
Titanic nearly collides with the drifting liner *New York*.

5:30 P.M.
Titanic anchors between the port breakwaters at Cherbourg, France.

requirement. Boat drills were to be conducted by the crew after the *Titanic* had left Southampton. Captain Smith had actually scheduled one to take place on the morning of April 14—the day his ship would strike an iceberg—but it was cancelled without explanation.

CROSSING TO CHERBOURG

Tugs eased the mighty *Titanic* from its berth at Southampton, and it began its journey to New York, stopping at Cherbourg, France, and Queenstown (now Cobh), Ireland, to pick up more passengers.

Left: *The maiden voyage of the* Titanic *was to be Captain Edward Smith's last voyage before he retired.*

Below: *A painting showing the* Titanic *leaving Southampton, England, on its journey to France.*

"My Dearest Bert . . . this is a tremendous boat. How I would love you to see it and explore it with me. . . . I have my ring now and kiss it every little while and think of you. I will drop you a card as soon as I reach land. God bless you, and write me soon. With love, Annie."
Letter written by third-class passenger Mary Anne Perrault to her fiancé, Bert Pickett, in London, April 10, 1912.

"My Dearest Bert, no doubt you have heard about the terrible disaster. I am surprised to have landed safe. It was an awful experience, not soon to be forgotten. I have only the clothes I stand in—and my ring."

Letter from Mary Anne Perrault, dated April 18, written on the rescue ship *Carpathia*. Eight months later, Mary Ann and Bert were married in Trenton, New Jersey. Chauffeur Bert had proposed the day before sailing—April 9, 1912—and given Mary Anne an engagement ring.

Above: *A pocket watch recovered from the wreck.*

Above: *The mangled wreck of HMS Hawke, which collided with the Olympic in September 1911.*

As the ship engaged its engines for the first time, the backwash from a propeller made the American liner *New York* pull against its moorings. The restraining ropes snapped, and the *New York* was free. A collision with the *Titanic* looked inevitable, but prompt action by the tugs averted mishap and separated the vessels. Some onlookers saw it as a bad omen, while others were reminded of claims that the great size of the *Titanic's* sister ship, the *Olympic*, had caused the HMS *Hawke* to similarly be drawn into a collision with it in September 1911. The excitement passed, however. By about 1:30 P.M. the *Titanic* had moved into the Solent, a small channel between England and the Isle of Wight, and was headed toward France. It arrived by early evening at Cherbourg, where 274 passengers were due to board the ship. Those arriving by train from Paris included 142 first-class passengers, most of them wealthy Americans. Among them were John Jacob Astor, reputedly the world's richest man, and his 19-year-old bride, Madeleine. Because the harbor at Cherbourg was not big enough for the *Titanic*, it anchored out at sea. A smaller ship, the *Nomadic*, was used to ferry out passengers and the mail that the gigantic liner was to carry across the Atlantic.

QUEENSTOWN: LAST SIGHT OF LAND
Shortly before noon on Thursday, the *Titanic* arrived on schedule at Queenstown, Ireland, where an excited crowd was gathered. The port was a busy place, handling around 30,000 Irish emigrants a year. Ironically, on the day the latest wave of Irish emigrants was preparing to leave their country, a third home rule bill was being introduced in the British Parliament. The bill proposed giving a measure of self-government to Ireland, with the hope of stemming the tide of Irish emigration. To mark this new hope, steerage passenger Eugene Daly of

Left: *From Southampton, the Titanic crossed to Cherbourg, shown here. The ship anchored offshore, and the tenders Nomadic and Traffic brought more passengers on board.*

Athlone, Ireland, played the patriotic Irish song "A Nation Once Again" on his bagpipes as passengers boarded. Like Cherbourg, Queenstown did not have a dock large enough to handle the ship, so the *Titanic* was anchored off Roche's Point, about 2 miles (3 km) from the coast. Two boats ferried 123 mainly third-class passengers to the ship. They were heading for what they hoped would

Above: *The* Titanic *waits outside Queenstown (now Cobh), Ireland, to pick up more passengers.*

be a new life in New York. More than 1,300 sacks of mail and 41 parcel hampers were also collected. The *Titanic* was not packed to capacity on her maiden voyage; third class, for example, was less than two-thirds full, but the White Star Line also made profits from carrying mail.

Left: *John Jacob Astor, said to be the world's wealthiest man, boarded the* Titanic *with his pregnant wife, 19-year-old Madeleine.*

TIME LINE
April 11

6:45 A.M.
Titanic passes Land's End, England, bound for Ireland.

9 A.M.
Hours before *Titanic* is due to arrive, people assemble near Queenstown harbor to catch a glimpse of the latest triumph of ship construction.

12:15 P.M.
Titanic drops anchor near the lighthouse at Roche's Point.

1:55 P.M.
Anchor is weighed as *Titanic* leaves last European landfall.

2:15 P.M.
British Army officer John Morrogh snaps the last photograph of the *Titanic*.

"This is a huge ship. Unless lots of people get on in Cherbourg and Queenstown they'll never half fill it. The dining-room is low-ceilinged but full of little tables for 2, 3 and more in secluded corners. How I wish someone I liked was on board, but then nice people do not sit at tables for two unless they're engaged or married. I wonder my blue blood didn't tell me that?

We nearly had a collision to start with. Coming out of Southampton we passed close to a ship that was tied up alongside the *Oceanic*, and the suction of our ship drew her out into the stream, and snapped the bonds that held her, and round she swung across our bows!

She had no steam up; so had to be pulled back by tugs, and we had to reverse. The name of her was the *New York*, in case you see it in the papers. It proves conclusively the case of the *Hawke* and *Olympic*."

Letter from first-class passenger Edward Pomeroy Colley to his cousin, April 10, 1912. Five days later, on his 37th birthday, Colley lost his life in the sinking.

Above: *The colorful Irish port of Cobh, formerly called Queenstown.*

Below: *A crewman watches as the Titanic prepares to leave Queenstown.*

Before the *Titanic* set off again, some of the lookouts began to question the ship's officers about the lack of binoculars, but the situation was never resolved. At 1:30 P.M. the starboard anchor was raised for the last time, and the *Titanic* departed on her first transatlantic crossing. Ironically, as *Titanic* left Queenstown, the ship that was eventually to come to its rescue, the *Carpathia*, was setting off from New York.

LUCKY ESCAPES

For a handful of fortunate first-class passengers, the journey ended when they disembarked at Queenstown. Another lucky person, fireman John Coffey, decided at the last minute to go home to his mother. He hid himself under mailbags on a tender going ashore. Coffey lived to the age of 68.

SETTLING ON BOARD

More than 2,200 people were now aboard the *Titanic*, including 1,300 passengers. More than 30 nationalities were represented on board, including about 120 Irish passengers, 63 Finns, 26 Swedes, and 245 Belgians. A Mrs. Ella White injured herself boarding at Cherbourg and took to her cabin, but most of the other passengers were eager to explore. Some of the many attractions included the Turkish baths, at a cost of around 4 shillings ($1), and the gymnasium with its electric camel, an undulating machine designed to strengthen the muscles. Those who chose to rent a deck chair for 4 shillings ($1) for the

"Our Queenstown representative was one of the privileged few who had the honour of meeting Captain Smith on the upper deck of the *Titanic* on Thursday last, just outside his apartment underneath the elevated bridge of this massive steamer, previous to his departure from Queenstown.

"I warmly complimented the veteran commander on his promotion to the largest steamship in the world. Captain Smith . . . quietly remarked that he fully realised his responsible position in having the command of such a luxurious ship with her immense number of passengers.

"As he paced the deck of his noble vessel getting everything in readiness for his westward passage, he presented a fine appearance, clad as he was in his commander's blue uniform. . . . [W]ith a well-trimmed beard and standing six feet [1.8 m] in height, he made a lasting impression on your correspondent. Shaking my hand warmly, he bade goodbye and sent his kind regards to friends on shore."

From the *Cork Free Press*, April 18, 1912.

Above: *A painting portraying Irish emigration to the United States. Many of the Irish passengers on board the Titanic were making a one-way trip.*

9 A.M.
Crew lifeboat assignment lists posted. Most do not read them.

10 A.M.
The captain leads his officers in a thorough inspection of ship.

Noon
Titanic has traveled 386 miles (621 km) since leaving Queenstown.

7 P.M.
Titanic receives warning from *La Touraine* about two thick ice fields ahead.

Above: *Irish piper Eugene Daly treated his fellow passengers to a tune on bagpipes like these as the Titanic waited for passengers to board in Queenstown.*

Above: *Over one thousand sacks of mail were brought on board the Titanic in Ireland.*

The desertion of stoker John Coffey made the news in light of the *Titanic*'s fate. The *Cork Examiner* reported that he had "a lucky escape" from being among those lost on the *Titanic*. It said that on the passage to Queenstown he had "decided to get out of her, as he did not relish his job."

A fellow fireman, survivor John Podesta, later recalled: "Coffey said to me, 'Jack, I'm going down to this tender to see my mother.' He asked me if anyone was looking and I said no, and bade him good luck. A few seconds later, he was gone!"

Other newspaper reports later claimed Coffey left because he "felt sure something was going to happen." Three days later, he joined the crew of the Cunard Line's *Mauretania* during her call at Queenstown. Family lore says he told New Yorkers on arriving that he had had a dream of the *Titanic* sinking, so left the ship.

Above: *This set of playing cards was recovered from the wreck of the Titanic and is now part of an exhibition in Memphis, Tennessee.*

voyage were continuously passed by those taking the air on the promenade deck.

SOCIAL ACTIVITIES

So stately was the mighty ship that few below deck had any sense of being at sea. More than once, passengers were heard to remark: "You would never imagine you were on a ship." A lively social life had sprung up almost immediately on board the *Titanic*, structured around the class system. Second-class passenger Lawrence Beesley, a British school teacher, looked down fondly from second class

at steerage passengers toward the stern who were engaged in an "uproarious skipping game." Grand music played in first class. A bugler summoned patrons to dinner with a few bars from "The Roast Beef of Old England." After dinner, many people sat in the beautiful first-class lounge and listened to the White Star orchestra play.

THE WIRELESS SYSTEM

Those feeling homesick could send a Marconi wireless telegram to loved ones, at a cost of 12 shillings and sixpence (about $4) for the first ten words. The wireless system was also valuable to the crew, since it transmitted information about conditions at sea. The captain and crew were therefore concerned when the wireless apparatus suddenly broke down on the night of April 13. Wireless operators stayed up all night and had it repaired by the early hours of Sunday, April 14. No one was aware at this stage how much they would soon depend on it for their lives.

"The rapid extension of the use of wireless telegraphy is shown by some figures in a report presented to the Conference (on wireless telegraphy at sea) by the German delegation. It appears that in the last four years, the number of ships, excluding warships, equipped with wireless telegraphy has increased from 52 to 926, and that during the same period the number of coast stations from 14 to 155."

From *The Times*, June 13, 1912. The *Titanic* tragedy helped illustrate the value of wireless technology in emergencies.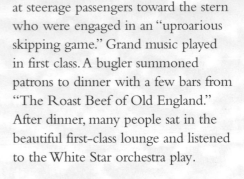

Above: An advertising poster for soap showing the Titanic ocean liner, which provided the soap for its first-class passengers.

Left: This telegraph machine from the Titanic was on the stern bridge and was probably part of the communication system linking the bridge to the engine room. This system was used to transmit orders for maneuvering the ship.

TIME LINE
April 13-14

10:30 A.M., April 13
Captain Smith informed that the bunker fire in boiler room six has finally been extinguished.

Noon, April 13
Notices posted show that a distance of 519 miles (835 km) has been covered since Friday.

11 P.M., April 13
Titanic's wireless apparatus breaks down.

5 A.M., April 14
Titanic's wireless is back in working order.

Above: Fine silverware recovered from the Titanic wreck.

Left: An artist's impression of the first-class dining room on board all of the White Star's liners.

"Our Boulogne correspondent writes that one of the last vessels to sight the *Titanic* was probably the *Boulogne* steamer trawler Alsace. . . . The trawler appears to have been rather dangerously near to the *Titanic*, passing so close in fact that she was splashed with spray from the *Titanic*'s bow. The fishermen cheered the liner, and their salutations were responded to by the officer on the bridge."

From *The Times*, April 22, 1912.

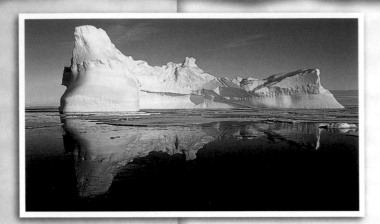

Above: Icebergs are dangerous obstacles for ships: only 10 percent of an iceberg's mass is visible above the water, and many bergs are strong enough to tear sheet metal.

Below: Captain Smith was not on the bridge when the Titanic struck the iceberg; he was alerted by the sound of the collision.

T he atmosphere on board the Titanic on Sunday morning was calm and relaxed. Despite receiving a number of ice warnings, the crew seemed unconcerned, and a planned inspection of the lifeboats was scrapped by Captain Smith for unknown reasons. Amazingly, it was not a legal requirement for the crew to carry out these inspections, and it was not required that passengers be assigned to lifeboats. By the end of the day, when the Titanic struck a giant iceberg, this lack of planning would only add to the chaos.

ICE AHEAD

The *Titanic's* communication room received several ice warnings on Sunday morning. At 9 A.M., an ice warning was received from the ship *Caronia,* and Officer Lightoller posted it in the chart room. At 11:40 A.M., the Dutch liner *Noordam* sent a message warning of "much ice" in the same location. Further ice warnings were received from the White Star Liner *Baltic* and a German liner called *Amerika.* Captain Smith passed the former on to J. Bruce Ismay, his managing director, who did not hand it back to him until the evening. In the

early evening, a message was received from the *Californian*, which was just 50 miles (80 km) northwest of the *Titanic*, and delivered to the bridge. The message warned of three big icebergs in the vicinity. Captain Smith, however, was not notified because he was attending a party held in his honor by the Wideners, a wealthy American family. On the bridge, officers were expecting to meet loose ice some time after 9 P.M. Smith visited the bridge at around 9:20 P.M. and asked to be notified if the weather changed. Tragically, an advice message from the *Mesaba* warning of a "great

"We had smooth seas, clear, starlit nights, fresh favouring winds; nothing to mar our pleasure. On Saturday, as Mr. Douglas and I were walking forward, we saw a seaman taking the temperature of the water. The deck seemed so high above the sea I was interested to know if the tiny pail could reach it. There was quite a breeze, and although the pail was weighted, it did not. This I watched from the open window of the covered deck. Drawing up the pail, the seaman filled it with water from the stand pipe, placed the thermometer in it, and went with it to the officer in charge."

American first-class passenger Mahala Douglas. The water temperature was recorded every two hours as a guide to changing ocean currents and conditions.

Right: *Captain Smith spent the afternoon with the Widener family in a first-class suite like the one shown here.*

Below: *The White Star Line's managing director, J. Bruce Ismay, was on board the* Titanic.

9 A.M.
Titanic receives warning from *Caronia* of bergs, growlers, and field ice in its track.

11:30 A.M.
Scheduled boat drill is cancelled, possibly due to high winds.

Noon
Titanic has run 546 miles (878 km) in the last 24 hours.

1:30 P.M.
Second-class purser Reginald Barker tells passenger Lawrence Beesley that the ship's speed is a disappointment.

11 P.M. (approximately)
Titanic is informed by *Californian*, now 35 miles (56 km) to the northwest, that it is stopped and "surrounded by ice." *Titanic* rebuffs message.

11:40 P.M.
Titanic, traveling at 22 knots (about 25 miles per hour), grazes an iceberg on her starboard side.

number of large icebergs" directly ahead never reached the *Titanic*. Then just after 11 P.M., the *Titanic's* wireless operator, Jack Phillips, had another conversation with Cyril Evans, the wireless operator of the *Californian*. Evans said his ship was "surrounded by ice," but Phillips ignored this warning, telling Evans to "shut up" because he was "busy." At 11:40 P.M., lookouts Fred Fleet and Reginald Lee were suddenly confronted with a dark object. The telephone rang on the bridge: "Iceberg, dead ahead!" First Officer William Murdoch had already spotted the obstacle. He yelled orders to reverse engines and to put the wheel hard-over to port. The *Titanic* seemed to be

"Just at that time I happened to be right in front of the crow's nest. My mate was telephoning, and I was standing in the front of the nest watching the berg.

"It was higher than the forecastle; but I could not say what height was clear of the water. It was a dark mass that came through that haze and there was no white appearing until it was just close alongside the ship, and that was just a fringe at the top.

"One side of it seemed to be black, and the other side seemed to be white. When I had a look at it going astern, it appeared to be white. She hit us. Close up against the side of the ship on the starboard bow.

"The ship seemed to heel slightly over to port as she struck the berg. Very slightly over to port, as she struck along the starboard side."

Titanic **lookout Reginald Lee in a statement during the British inquiry.**

Above: *The ship's wheel has laid rusting at the bottom of the ocean for more than ninety years.*

Right: *A telephone from the after-docking bridge. It would have been used to send messages to the engine room or the navigating bridge.*

inching toward escape before it plunged into the iceberg, accompanied by a screeching sound of buckling metal. Captain Smith ordered the engines to be stopped in order to inspect damage. Initially, Fourth Officer Joseph Boxhall reported that he could not see any damage, but carpenter John Maxwell, sent below to inspect (and possibly repair) any damage, reported that water was coming into the ship.

CALLING FOR HELP

Captain Smith sent for shipbuilder and chief design engineer Thomas Andrews. Discovering that the ship was letting in water through the bow section and at least three other compartments, Andrews told Captain Smith that the ship had probably less than ninety minutes before it sank. There were 2,200 people on board, but the twenty emergency craft on the *Titanic* could carry only about 1,200 people. It was now 12:10 A.M. Captain Smith fired out a chain of orders. All lifeboats were urgently uncovered, all crew reported for

"The captain came in to the operating room. He told us that we had better get assistance. When Mr. Phillips [Jack Phillips, senior operator] heard him, he came out [of the room where he had gone to sleep] and asked if he wanted him to use a distress call.

"[The captain] said, 'Yes; at once.' The message was sent immediately . . . CQD about half a dozen times; MGY half a dozen times. [CQD is a recognized international distress call; MGY is the code call of the *Titanic*.]

"I could read what Mr. Phillips was sending, but I could not get the answers because he had the telephones. . . . He told me to go to the captain and report the *Frankfurt*. He was in communication with the *Frankfurt* and had our position.

"I delivered that message to the captain. . . . He wanted to know where she was, her latitude and longitude, I told him we would get that as soon as we could."

Testimony of wireless operator Harold Bride during the U.S. Senate inquiry. A ship's position is marked by degrees latitude and longitude.

Above: *A scene from the film* Titanic *(1997), showing how quickly the ship filled up with water after impact.*

TIME LINE
April 15

12:15 A.M.
Titanic sends first distress message, giving an estimated position of north latitude 41.46° and longitude 50.24° west.

12:25 A.M.
Ship's position corrected to north latitude 41.46° and longitude 50.14° west. Call from *Titanic* received by *Carpathia* says: "Come at once. We have struck a berg."

12:26 A.M.
Crew tamps down fires in the boilers to cool them before contact with water. Steam noisily blows out of the funnels.

12:30 A.M.
Titanic to *Frankfurt*: "Tell your captain to come to our help. We are on the ice."

12:35 A.M.
Lights of an unknown ship seen by people on *Titanic*. *Titanic* fires rockets.

12:45 A.M.
First lifeboat, number 7 on the starboard side, is launched.

duty, and passengers were brought up on deck. Women and children were to board the lifeboats first. Everyone had to put on a life belt, while an emergency distress message was transmitted to summon all available assistance before the ship sank. The message, sent by wireless operators Jack Phillips and Harold Bride, read: "CQD, MGY:41.46° N 50.14° W. We have struck a berg. Require assistance. Putting the women off in boats."

Above: *This wrench was one of the tools used by the engineers who worked hard to keep the Titanic's pumps and lights working.*

"My wife and I were awakened by the shock to the vessel. Listening a moment, I became aware that the engines had been stopped, and shortly afterwards, hearing hurried footsteps on the ship deck, directly over our stateroom, I concluded that I would go out and inquire what had occurred. Partially dressing, I slipped out of our room into the forward companionway, there to find possibly half a dozen men, all speculating as to what had happened. While we stood there an officer passed by somewhat hurriedly, and I asked him what was the trouble; he replied that he thought something had gone wrong with the propeller, but that it was nothing serious.

"Leaving the few passengers that I had observed still laughing and chatting, I returned to my stateroom. My wife, being somewhat uneasy, desired to arise and dress. I informed my wife what the officer had told me. . . . I decided, nevertheless, to again go out and investigate further."

First-class passenger Dr. Washington Dodge in a speech to the Commonwealth Club, May 11, 1912.

Above: An artist's impression of the Titanic's sinking.

E ven when they realized that the Titanic had collided with an iceberg, many passengers were reluctant to leave the ship. Some believed the myth that had grown up around the ship—that it was unsinkable—while others were justifiably terrified of being cast out onto the dark and freezing sea in simple lifeboats. This hesitation meant that valuable time was wasted, and many of the ship's lifeboats went away half empty. When another ship seemed to be approaching in the distance, persuading passengers to leave became even more difficult.

Above: An artist's impression of the Titanic's lifeboats being lowered.

A LOST SAVIOR

While the *Titanic* continued to fill up with water, a ship sighted in the distance offered a measure of comfort to those on board. Norwegian passenger Olaus Abelseth, 26, reported seeing the light plainly from the *Titanic's* port side. He noted, "A little while later there was one of the officers who came and said to be quiet, there was a ship coming." Captain Smith desperately ordered the crew in lifeboat eight to row to the mystery ship and make it return with them to the *Titanic*. Fourth Officer Boxhall fired rockets to attract

attention. He was joined by two quartermasters, who also fired rockets, yet the ship refused to continue toward the *Titanic*. A misguided hope that the mystery ship might rescue the *Titanic*, coupled with a reluctance to leave the ship, meant that many of the spaces on the *Titanic's* lifeboats went empty. The first lifeboat lowered, boat seven, had room for 65 people, yet just 28 people boarded. Boat five was lowered with 24 spaces left unfilled. Boat one left with just 12 of its 40 places filled, and boat eight had 39 out of its 65 spaces filled. Lifeboat four left with room for 25 more people on board. Two of the collapsible lifeboats were eventually swept away, but some people were saved after they managed to climb on top of one of the capsized boats.

DEATH OF A MAIDEN

Back on board the *Titanic*, the news reaching Captain Smith was increasingly bleak. There was no hope of containing the flooding: It had already filled the first two boiler

"As one of the lifeboats was being filled with women and children, a foreigner tried to jump in the boat. The officer told him to go on deck. He refused, and the officer fired, and the man fell dead on deck. The crowd of foreigners who were hanging around the lifeboat cowed back when they found one of their countrymen dead.

"The lifeboat was lowered, and the officer kept on firing his revolver until he was level with the water. I saw a similar instance occur on the port side. A passenger tried to claim a seat in one of the boats. The officer told him to leave at once, and as he hesitated, a revolver shot was fired, and he dropped dead in the water."

Mess Steward C. W. Fitzpatrick, quoted in the *Northern Constitution*, May 4, 1912.

12:55 A.M.
Lifeboats 5 and 6 launched on opposite sides of *Titanic*.

1 A.M.
Lifeboat 3 launched. Crewmen still "all standing about," according to fireman Alfred Shiers who left in 3. "They did not think it was serious."

1:10 A.M.
Lifeboat 8 told to row for the light on the port side. Lifeboat 1 departs from the starboard side with only twelve occupants.

1:25 A.M.
Olympic asks her sister ship: "Are you steering southerly to meet us?" *Titanic* replies: "We are putting the women off in boats."

Above: *Unlike this artist's depiction, the Titanic's hull is believed to have split in half before the ship sank completely.*

rooms and the steerage accommodations in the bow, along with the post office and squash court. Because the bulkheads separating the ship's compartments only went up as high as D-deck, the water

Fourth Officer Boxhall: "My attention until the time I left the ship was mostly taken up with firing off distress rockets and trying to signal a steamer that was almost ahead of us. I saw his masthead lights and I saw his side light. By the way she was heading, she seemed to be meeting us, coming toward us."

U.S. Senate inquiry chairman Senator William Smith: "Do you know anything about what boat that was?" Boxhall: "No, sir."

Smith: "Have you had any information since about it?" Boxhall: "None whatever."

Smith: "You say you fired these rockets and otherwise attempted to signal her?"

Boxhall: "Yes, sir. She got close enough, as I thought, to read our electric Morse signal, and I signalled to her; I told her to come at once, we were sinking."

"I told the Captain about this ship, and he was with me most of the time when we were signalling. I went over and started the Morse signal. He said, 'Tell him to come at once, we are sinking.'"

Testimony of Fourth Officer Boxhall during the U.S. Senate inquiry on the *Titanic*'s sinking.

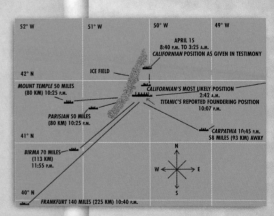

Above: *Map pinpointing the Titanic's exact position when it found itself in trouble and the distance of the nearest ships to the stricken vessel.*

Above: *A gold wristwatch found in the first-class section of the ship. More first-class passengers made it to safety than passengers in any other class.*

Below: *Captain Arthur Henry Rostron of the Cunard's Mauretania, is shown here in his uniform as aide-de-camp to the King of England, the highest mark of recognition open to his profession. While in command of the Carpathia, Captain Rostron was awarded the U.S. Congressional Gold Medal for his bravery in rescuing the survivors of the Titanic disaster.*

overflowed at D–Deck and rushed down palatial corridors into new sections of the vessel.

At 1:20 A.M. the engineers called off their efforts to pump water from the ship. They were ordered on deck and told to equip themselves with life belts. (They did not, as some myths claim, remain at their posts until they were swallowed by the sea.) By now, the *Titanic* was visibly slumping deeper in the water, and on deck complacency was replaced by terror. Departed lifeboats failed to respond to megaphone calls that they return to

the ship to take on more passengers. The panic led to gunshots, fired in the air to stop rushes at the remaining boats. Later, at official inquiries, no one admitted to seeing anyone killed by gunfire, but witnesses reported some shootings to the press. Finally, all the lifeboats were gone, and at 2:20 A.M. the *Titanic* sank.

RESCUE AND RETURN

It was after 4 A.M. when the Cunard liner *Carpathia*, responding to the *Titanic's* distress call, reached the area. The first lifeboat the *Carpathia* found was lifeboat two, which contained Fourth Officer Joseph Boxhall. Boxhall reported to the *Carpathia's* captain, Arthur Rostron, the exact time of the *Titanic's* sinking. Meanwhile, other exhausted survivors were hauled on board. Rostron cancelled his voyage to Europe and headed for New York with some 711 survivors. Questions were being asked even before the *Carpathia* arrived in New York. How could a major liner make such a long journey with so few lifeboats? Why were there so many empty places in the lifeboats when they were finally launched? And why was the *Titanic* going so fast at night in reported ice? In the absence of many firm facts, the waiting press

"Captain Rostron, the commander of the Cunard liner *Carpathia,* was today presented with a cheque for $10,000, raised by [U.S.] public subscription. . . .

"Acknowledging the cheque, Captain Rostron declared that he would never forget the way in which he had been received by Americans, though he again maintained that the members of his crew were entitled to equal credit. 'I shall use this cheque,' he said, 'for the education of my three sons, whom I hope to bring up as worthy representatives of the Anglo-Saxon race.' "

From the *New York World*, June 4, 1912.

"Captain Smith stood next to me as we got in [to lifeboat 8], and told Tom Jones, a sailor who acted nobly, to row straight for those ship lights over there, land the passengers aboard, and return as soon as possible.

"For three hours we pulled steadily for the lights seen three miles [4.8 km] away; then we saw a port light vanish and the masthead lights grow dimmer until they disappeared."

Nöelle, Countess of Rothes, in an interview in the *Journal of Commerce*, April 1912.

engaged in speculation and sensationalism. The press inferred from the known lists of survivors that first-class men behaved nobly by giving up their lives and lifeboat places to the "weaker sex"— women—and defenseless children. The press also concluded that steerage passengers had behaved in a hysterical, cowardly fashion, jeopardizing lifeboats in their panic. The "better" class of people must have fended them off, noted some reports, and the crew had been obliged to shoot. By the time *Carpathia* arrived, rumors put forth various notions, including the ideas that the band had played the hymn "Nearer, My God, to Thee" as the ship sank and that cowards had escaped dressed in women's clothing.

WHO WAS TO BLAME?

The U.S. Senate and later the British Board of Trade carried out official investigations into the

Above: *The mystery of exactly how the ship went under was not solved until the 1980s.*

Below Right: *The Titanic was equipped with enough lifeboats to rescue 53 percent of its passengers, but only 32 percent were saved. This boat was one of the few that left fully filled.*

TIME LINE
April 15

1:45 A.M.
Last signals from *Titanic* heard by *Carpathia*, rushing to the rescue but still hours away. "Engine room full up to boilers."

1:50 A.M.
Lifeboats 2, 9, 10, 11, 12, 13, 14, 15, and 16 have all left. Only five boats remain.

1:55 A.M.
Lifeboat 4 is launched. Captain Smith tells wireless officers that they have done their full duty.

2 A.M.
White Star Line Managing Director J. Bruce Ismay leaves in collapsible boat C. Hundreds, including women and children, remain.

2:05 A.M.
Collapsible boat D leaves. Other passengers attempt to free collapsible boats A and B from the roof of the officer quarters.

2:20 A.M.
Boat A is swept off, water-logged; boat B capsized by waves. *Titanic* sinks.

"The disproportion between the numbers of the passengers saved in the first, second, and third classes is due to various causes, among which the difference in the position of their quarters and the fact that many of the third-class passengers were foreigners are perhaps the most important. The disproportion was certainly not due to any discrimination by the officers or crew in assisting the passengers to the boats. The disproportion between the numbers of the passengers and crew saved is due to the fact that the crew, for the most part, all attended to their duties to the last, and until all the boats were gone."

Number of passengers saved per class:

First class	203 out of 325, or 62.46%.
Second class	118 out of 285, or 41.40%.
Third class	178 out of 706, or 25.21%.
Crew	212 out of 885, or 23.95%.
Total saved	711 out of 2,201, or 32.30%.

From the British inquiry's final report, July, 1912.

Above: *Cover of a newspaper running an account of the Titanic disaster.*

Below: *J. Bruce Ismay (far right), managing director of the White Star Line, and his wife arrive at an inquiry following the Titanic disaster. The general manager of the White Star Line is shown on the left.*

circumstances surrounding the sinking of the *Titanic*. The investigations arrived at very different conclusions. In the United States, the mood toward the crew was hostile, with the *New York Herald* lamenting that "so many American lives were wasted by the incompetency of British seamen." Forty-three crew members were detained in New York and ordered to give evidence at the U.S. Senate's inquiry. The Senate held Captain Smith fully responsible for traveling too fast in such treacherous conditions. The British inquiry, however, decided that speeding in the vicinity of ice did not amount to reckless navigation, after hearing evidence that it was common practice among liners seeking to meet tight schedules. The board ruled that the tragedy had provided a warning and that similar behavior in light of what had happened would constitute negligence. More controversially, both the U.S. and British inquiries concluded that the lights seen by the sinking *Titanic* had belonged to the freighter *Californian*. This vessel had seen rockets, undoubtedly from the *Titanic*, but its officers had been unsure of what the rockets signified. The rockets were "low-lying," yet the officers linked them to another ship a few miles away. The *Californian* was actually about 20 miles (32 km) to the north when the *Titanic* was sinking.

REFORMS

Original plans for the *Titanic* included forty-eight lifeboats, but in the end it had only twenty. This number, however, was still more than the number of lifeboats required by government regulations. The regulations were outdated; they had not been changed since 1894, when the largest vessel on the water was less than a quarter of the *Titanic's* size. After the tragedy, the law was changed to ensure there was lifeboat capacity for everyone on board, and all ships at sea were compelled by law to monitor their wirelesses continuously for any distress signals. All ships carrying more than one hundred passengers were also required to have a watertight inner hull. History suggests that the lessons of the *Titanic* were quickly learned. Just ten days after it sank, coal stokers on board its sister ship, the *Olympic*,

Above: Marcelle Navratil of Nice traveled to New York to be reunited with her children, who survived the Titanic's sinking. Their father went down with the ship.

went on strike because the ship did not have enough lifeboats. Although the strikers were arrested, the *Olympic's* voyage was cancelled. When *Titanic's* second sister ship, the *Britannic*, struck a mine just four years later, it sank in approximately 55 minutes, but this time only 30

"One of the most romantic mysteries of the *Titanic* tragedy is that of two little waifs, aged four and two years, who were rescued from the wreck. Miss Margaret Hays, a young woman of wealth and culture, took the children to the beautiful home of her father, where they were cared for. Now the mystery is solved. The names of the children are Michel and Edmond Navratil, of Nice, and their pet names are Lolo and Momon. Their father, with whom they were travelling to America on board the *Titanic*, married 17-year old Marcelle Collata. Two lovely boys were born to them, but petty disagreements arose and a year ago they agreed to separate. The father got possession of the boys and started with them for America under the assumed named of Hoffman. When the *Titanic's* lifeboats were being filled, he came forward and placed his sons in one, but stepped back and went down with the ship."

From the *Christian Herald*, June 5, 1912.

people lost their lives. A further legacy of the *Titanic* disaster was the establishment of an International

"We knew nothing until the *Carpathia* docked, and all sorts of weird rumours were afloat as she came to her pier. One was that she was bringing about 300 dead; another was of panic and shooting while filling the lifeboats.

"As soon as the passengers got off the *Carpathia* and the survivors began to come ashore, a large number of them made a bee-line to the various newspaper offices to tell the story of the wreck and how they were rescued—fixing their price first. Some of them had photos, too. As you know, the fact that J. Bruce Ismay came safely to shore while a lot of his passengers were left to drown caused a lot of talk.

"Hearst's papers have been full of vituperation and abuse for him, printing his name in large type under his picture ' J. Brute Ismay.' They also had a cartoon of him in a lifeboat full of women, looking like a poor shivering coward."

New York Herald staffer J. Norman Lynd in a letter, April 1912.

TIME LINE
April 1912

April 16
Early British newspaper editions claim *Titanic* is being towed to Halifax, Nova Scotia, Canada.

April 17
Carpathia makes it clear that it is the sole carrier of survivors.

April 18
Rescue vessel arrives in New York at night in a thunderstorm.

April 19
First sitting of the U.S. Senate Inquiry. J. Bruce Ismay is the first witness.

April 20
Wireless operator Harold Bride tells U.S. Senate that *Titanic* was repeatedly warned of ice.

April 21
Search ships *Minia* and *Mackay-Bennett* arrive in vicinity of bodies from the wreck.

April 22
Evidence shows that Marconi used the tragedy to gain publicity for his wireless technology.

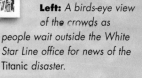

Left: *A birds-eye view of the crowds as people wait outside the White Star Line office for news of the Titanic disaster.*

Above: *Papers published tales of heroic engineers such as Arthur Ward who continued to work as the ship sank.*

It is almost impossible to overestimate the impact the sinking of the Titanic *had on the society of the day. Newspapers ran endless pieces on the disaster for a public whose appetite for the story was voracious. The tragedy was also told in music and later on television and in film. The enduring appeal of the story was demonstrated more recently by the worldwide success of the 1997 movie.*

NEWSPAPERS

Press reports after the *Titanic's* sinking reflected the public's various moods and emotions, including the national humiliation that quickly seized Great Britain after so appalling a loss. Myths were forged to make the reality more palatable—that the band nobly played hymns to the end, that the engineers remained at their posts until caught by torrents of water rushing in, and that the crew and men from first class behaved selflessly. No one felt it was in bad taste to print what were described as "thrilling" stories of the disaster. Newspapers ran campaigns to raise money for the widows and orphans left by the disaster. The press never quite let the story go and in the 1950s and 1960s still reported the deaths of survivors.

Left: *The sinking of the "unsinkable" Titanic continued to grab newspaper headlines across the world years after the event.*

"A committee has been formed for the purpose of arranging for the erection of a suitable memorial to the late Commander Edward John Smith RNR, the Captain of the *Titanic*.

"It is proposed that it should take the two-fold form of a monument with inset medallion at Lichfield, in the county where he was born, and of a stained glass window and tablet in the new Cathedral at Liverpool. Queen Alexandra has been graciously pleased to express her sympathy and interest in this project. Lord Pirrie is a member of the committee."

From *The Times*, September 27, 1913.

THE DISASTER IN MUSIC

The first piano selections to "honor the dead" appeared within weeks of the *Titanic's* demise. Some songs had better titles—and melodies—than others. One recording was entitled "Be British," supposedly after the captain's last words, while another bemoaned "The Ship That Will Never Return." A music sheet told how "My Sweetheart Went Down with the Ship," complete with a picture of a couple staring into one another's eyes on a sloping deck. In France, the song the ship's band was supposedly playing as the *Titanic* went down— "Nearer, my God, to Thee"—was quickly translated into French; 50,000 copies of the French translation, "Plus près de toi, mon Dieu," sold in less than a week. In the United States, the sinking became the subject of songs known as Negro spirituals. Although there were few black people aboard, the theme had a distinct appeal and led eventually to a popular campfire song, "It Was Sad When the Ship Went Down." In late 1997, the signature song of the movie *Titanic*, "My Heart Will Go On" by Celine Dion, became a worldwide hit. Ironically it helped to sow fresh interest in the actual music played on the *Titanic*, and spin-off recordings flourished—winning new fans of classical music.

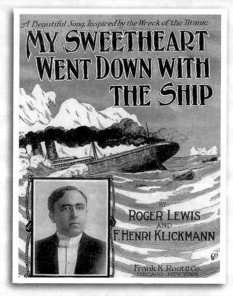

Above: *The cover of a popular piece of sheet music, "My Sweetheart Went Down with the Ship."*

FILM AND TELEVISION

Movies were made almost immediately after the sinking of the *Titanic*. One dramatic treatment appeared on film within a few weeks of the disaster and starred actress Dorothy Gibson, who had been a first-class passenger who survived the sinking. World War I served to push the story from the public's mind, but it reemerged in a 1929 movie, *Atlantic*, which the White Star Line immediately denounced as a slur on British shipping. In 1938, the great

film director Alfred Hitchcock announced plans for a feature production of the story, but World War II intervened. During the war, when Germany and Great Britain were enemies, a German version of the disaster portrayed the British on board as incompetent cowards. In 1955, Walter Lord's

ECHO OF *TITANIC* DISASTER

"Paris, France—So much attention has been attracted in France by the incident of the *Titanic's* band playing the hymn "Nearer, my God, to Thee" when the vessel was going down that a cheap edition of the French translation, entitled "Plus près de toi, mon Dieu," has been published, and in less than one week 50,000 copies have been sold at one penny each. The hymn is even being sung by groups at street corners after the manner of popular songs."

From *Reuters*, May 13, 1912.

TIME LINE
1912–1919

May 15, 1912
Lord Mayor of London closes his *Titanic* fund as it reaches £262,000 ($140,000).

May 24, 1912
Titanic band tribute in London. Nearly 500 musicians, "the greatest professional orchestra ever assembled," play.

April 15, 1913
Titanic memorial lighthouse opened in New York.

April 29, 1914
Engineers' Memorial unveiled in Southampton.

July 29, 1914
Statue unveiled to Captain Smith in Lichfield, England.

1915
Eastland sinking in Chicago is allegedly caused by top-heaviness from the addition of lifeboats for all passengers; 884 lives lost.

Left: *Canadian singer Celine Dion's song "My Heart Will Go On" was the theme song for the film* Titanic *(1997). The song was a worldwide hit.*

A NIGHT TO REMEMBER

WALTER LORD

Above: *The film A Night to Remember (1956) inspired fresh interest in the Titanic disaster.*

book, *A Night to Remember,* inspired a major revival of interest in the disaster, and a film of the same name, starring Kenneth More as Second Officer Lightoller, followed a year later with great success. The discovery of the wreck in 1985 led to new TV programs, including one in which actor Telly Savalas opened a recovered *Titanic* safe in a 1987 live broadcast to discover not jewels but a mass of sodden papers. In 1997, the James Cameron movie *Titanic* captured the public imagination once more. The set consisted of half

of a replica ship built in Baja, Mexico, with the Pacific Ocean, rather than the Atlantic, as the backdrop. More than three hours long, it starred British actress Kate Winslet and American actor Leonardo DiCaprio. The film won eleven Oscars and was the first film to gross more than $1 billion worldwide. Viewers were seduced by the film's fictional love story, and computer-generated animation gave a detailed account of how the ship probably sank. Spin-offs included 3-D movies on the state of the wreck, a documentary on Cameron's visit to the site, and the IMAX 3-D movie *Ghosts of the Abyss* (2003).

TITANIC ON CANVAS

From the moment construction of the great ship began, it inspired those interested in the visual arts.

"Some jump, some fall, each dotting the water's surface like the period at the end of a sentence. Then, the stern slips under the water, plunging everyone into a coldness so intense it is indistinguishable from fire. Ten minutes. Twenty minutes. The inchoate wail of fifteen hundred souls slowly fades to individual cries from the darkness. We know you can hear us! Save one life! Seven hundred survivors stand by in lifeboats built for twelve hundred, afraid to act for fear of getting swamped. They tell themselves that the voices from the water do not belong to their husbands or their loved ones. They are merely the cries of the damned."

From the screenplay to *Titanic*, directed by James Cameron for Paramount Pictures and Twentieth Century Fox. The movie became the highest-grossing film of the twentieth century, taking in more than $1 billion at the box office worldwide. It was also the most expensive movie ever made, costing $200 million.

"High in the crow's nest of the new White Star liner *Titanic*, Lookout Frederick Fleet peered into a dazzling night. It was calm, clear, and bitterly cold. There was no moon, but the cloudless sky blazed with stars. The Atlantic was like polished plate glass; people later said they had never seen it so smooth.

"This was the fifth night of the *Titanic's* maiden voyage to New York, and it was already clear that she was not only the largest but also the most glamorous ship in the world. Even the passengers' dogs were glamorous."

The opening lines of the classic *Titanic* book *A Night to Remember* by Walter Lord. The book prompted a whole new generation to begin researching the *Titanic*. Ironically, as people began researching, they discovered the book that had inspired them was littered with mistakes.

Left: *Plans for a Titanic film directed by the master of suspense Alfred Hitchcock sank with the outbreak of World War II.*

Above: The lifeboats are lowered in a scene from the film Titanic (1997).

1920
Titanic memorial unveiled in Belfast, Northern Ireland.

1928
The sinking of *Vestris* and various other peacetime tragedies at sea cause the press to invoke the *Titanic* as the worst of all.

1931
Captain Arthur Rostron, rescuer of *Titanic* survivors, publishes memoirs titled *Home from the Sea.*

1931
A life belt marked S.S. *Titanic* is reported washed up on the shore of Gravesend Bay, New York, in May.

Photographs of the ship were taken for postcards and for the shipyard's own publicity. The ship was also painted by artists working for the White Star Line. A painting done in 1912 by the acclaimed maritime artist Charles Dixon, titled *Titanic Being Fitted Out at Queen's Island, Belfast,* hangs in the Ulster Folk and Transport Museum. Since then, the ship has been painted by a host of amateur and professional artists. More recently, American artist Ken Marschall has painted the ship in realistic detail and has also painted images of how the wreck looks today.

TITANIC ON THE STAGE

Theatrical drama about the ship is much more scarce. In 1931, the ship had a cameo appearance in the play *Cavalcade* by Noël Coward. The play was turned into a movie a year later. Various musicals and other adaptations came and went, and many were panned by the critics. The stage musical *Titanic,* however, was a smash hit on Broadway when it debuted in 1997. A number of minor playwrights have mined dramatic material from the U.S. and British inquiries, including the Texan author Pat Cook and Belfast-based Denis MacNeice. MacNeice's play *Blackness After Midnight* focuses on Stanley Lord, captain of the *Californian,* the ship which may have been closest to the *Titanic* at the time of its sinking.

Below: The tale of the sunken supership has even reached the stage. Here, some of the cast from the musical Titanic wait to board the ship.

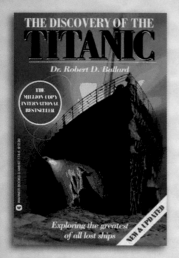

Above: *Dr. Robert Ballard, discoverer of the Titanic wreck, wrote a popular book about his work.*

A fter the Titanic *sank and the last of the survivors were hauled to safety, the grim task of recovering and burying the dead began. Today, graves for the* Titanic's *dead can be found throughout the world. The search for the ship itself began almost immediately after the disaster. The wreck, however, would remain undiscovered for more than seventy years.*

IDENTIFYING THE DEAD

In 1912, four small ships were sent to collect the remains of those who were lost. Fewer than 330 victims were recovered by the *Mackay-Bennett, Minia, Montmagny,* and *Algerine.* A significant number were reburied at sea after identification. Others lie in cemeteries near the search vessels' Canadian home port. In Halifax, Nova Scotia, a large plot of *Titanic* graves includes the stone of an Irish crewman J. Dawson. After the movie *Titanic* (1997) was released, this marker was festooned with flowers by those who believed it was the actual grave of Jack Dawson, the fictional character played by Leonardo DiCaprio. *Titanic* steward William Cheverton's body was discovered by the steamer *Ilford* on June 8, 1912, and buried at sea. His body was the last to be recovered. More recently, scientists have used new technology to identify some of the unidentified victims of the tragedy. DNA testing has revealed that the "unknown child" buried by crewmen of the *Mackay-Bennett* in Halifax in 1912 was Eino Panula, a 13-month-old Finnish boy.

THE DEATH SHIP AT HALIFAX
A Gruesome Spectacle

"The *Mackay-Bennett* reached port this morning and discharged her freight of 190 bodies, landing her sad burden occupying the whole day. Bodies lay in a great pyramid of coffins on deck, while others, uncoffined, were piled under tarpaulins. The latter were the first to be removed.

"When the coverings were first thrown back more than fifty bodies were disclosed to sight. They lay on their backs with the sunlight shining into their sightless eyes. Some bore an appearance of repose, but the features of others were contorted. Men with stretchers were quickly engaged in the work of removal. . . . the bodies were then taken in charge by the undertakers.

"These quickly placed the bodies in rough pine boxes and lifted them into black hearses which hastened off at the rate of one a minute.

"Many of the bodies were without clothing. According to the *Mackay-Bennett's* crew, none of the bodies bore bullet marks."

Press Association dispatch from Halifax, Nova Scotia, April 30, 1912.

Below: *On Thursday, April 17, the ship Mackay-Bennett steamed to the site of the Titanic's sinking to search for bodies. The first corpses were brought aboard on April 21.*

Above: On May 17, 2001, work crews in Halifax, Nova Scotia, exhumed the remains of three Titanic victims whose identities were unknown. Through DNA testing, the identities of some of the victims were discovered.

TIME LINE
1935–1990

1935
Second Officer Lightoller pens his account, *Titanic and Other Ships*.

1938
Hitchcock movie *Titanic*, slated to begin shooting; is eventually scrapped.

1953
First expedition to find the wreck mounted by salvage firm Risdon Beasley.

1962
Fiftieth anniversary marked. Death of Stanley Lord, whose *Californian* was wrongly identified as the nearby ship.

1985
A deep-towed sonar imaging system on *Knorr* research ship shows a giant boiler on ocean floor—the first sight of *Titanic* wreck.

SEARCHING FOR THE WRECK

Expeditionary voyages to find the *Titanic*'s wreckage were planned almost as soon as the ship sank. One firm contracted with a number of bereaved families in 1912 to locate the wreck, raise it, and recover their loved ones' remains. Predictably nothing came of it. In 1913, some widows organized a "pilgrimage" to the spot where it was believed the *Titanic* sank, and they scattered flowers on the waves. Over the years, searchers developed various schemes to find the wreckage. British salvage firm Risdon Beasley mounted a reconnaissance in the 1950s, and in 1977, a British submarine encountered a sonar hit on a large wreck that might have been the

Right: A map showing the Titanic's journey and the location of the wreck.

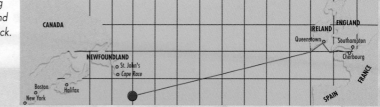

"About 12:30 on Tuesday we were playing shuffleboard on deck when we noticed our boat making a sharp turning movement. We could not make it out, and thought at first a derelict was in front, but after a few minutes we sighted the lifeboat in the water on our starboard [side].

"We passed within 50 yards [45 m] of it. By then our engines had been stopped, so we could plainly see the three men in it. It was the most pathetic sight I have ever witnessed. One man was lying under the bows and the other two in the stern. Their legs were under the thwarts, and this no doubt held them in the boat. They all had life belts on, and we could see their faces were almost black."

Letter from Harry Church of Birmingham, England. He was on the *Oceanic* on May 15, exactly one month after the tragedy, when the ship came upon the collapsible lifeboat A carrying abandoned bodies. It was 350 miles (560 km) from the site of the sinking.

Titanic. In 1980, Texan oil millionaire Jack Grimm poured millions of dollars into abortive expeditions that came up empty-handed. The search finally ended in 1985, when a French-American expedition found the exact spot of the wreck. Before the wreck was actually seen, however, someone in the British military establishment tipped off the *London Observer* newspaper that the *Titanic* had been found. The day the front-page story was printed—September 1, 1985—was the actual date that the remains of the *Titanic* came back into view for the first time in seventy-three years. Underwater imaging equipment aided the searchers. The expedition, led by Jean-Louis Michel and Robert Ballard, was funded by French and U.S. ocean science institutes. The world was electrified by the find. The discovery confirmed two facts: The ship had broken in two as it sank, contrary to the finding of the British inquiry, and it had not

been where it said it was in its SOS transmissions—- it was more than 13 miles (21 km) further east. This latter fact explained the failure to find it in earlier expeditions. It also confirmed the 1912 testimony from the *Californian* about where rockets had been seen. The British inquiry believed the SOS position was accurate and that the *Californian* observers had lied.

Below: *Dr. Robert Ballard on board a research vessel in 2004.*

Above: *A photograph of a chandelier from the* Titanic.

"I turned to Jean-Louis. The look in his eyes said everything. The *Titanic* had been found. We'd been right all along. Then he said softly, 'It was not luck. We earned it.'

"Our hunt was almost over. Somewhere very near us lay the RMS *Titanic.* . . . larger and larger pieces of wreckage were now passing under *Argo* and Earl had to winch in to avoid hitting them. We didn't yet know where the main wreckage was.

"As the images on the video screen grew more and more vivid—large pieces of twisted hull plating, portholes, a piece of railing turned on its side—for the first time since I had started on this quest twelve years before, the full human impact of the *Titanic's* terrifying tragedy began to sink in.

"Here at the bottom of the ocean lay not only the graveyard of a great ship, but the only fitting monument to the more than 1,500 people who had perished when she went down."

Dr. Robert D. Ballard, in his book *The Discovery of the* Titanic, Madison Publishing, 1987.

Above: A mini-submarine is sent down to visit the site of the wreck.

A CENTER OF INTEREST

Since its discovery, the wreck of the *Titanic*, laying 560 miles (900 km) from Newfoundland, has been the focus of dozens of expeditions. Tourists now can dive to see the wreck—for a cost of thousands of dollars a dive. Radio stations and other commercial interest groups have given away trips as prizes. Two people were even married on the wreck; David Leibowitz and Kimberley Miller exchanged vows in a mini-submarine resting on the submerged bow. Since the discovery, a debate has been raging on the salvage question. Thousands of items have been retrieved from the debris, despite the objections of some survivors and relatives of victims who point out that it is still a mass grave. Many of the items recovered—a tube of toothpaste, bottles of Bass ale—seem relatively ordinary, but they are compelling enough to draw

thousands to see various traveling exhibitions of recovered artifacts.

PRESERVATION EFFORTS

The condition of some recovered items has been little short of wondrous. Leather pouches preserved papers from the worst ravages of seawater while they lay on the seabed for decades. Most artifacts, however, have had to undergo painstaking scientific conservation efforts. Two laboratories in France have restored

"The discovery of the *Titanic* and re-awakening of interest has had many effects, from world-record prices of £50,000 sterling (about $266,000) for a menu from the ship and $100,000 for a baggage tag, to the advent of some 120 new books.

"One man claims to be the reincarnation of shipbuilder Thomas Andrews and has hindsight on the sinking. Another author insists there was no iceberg at all, and that the *Titanic* was ripped asunder in her keel by flat and low-lying ice.

"One thing is sure: the *Titanic* will eventually be wholly re-imagined, since the wreck is succumbing ever more steadily to the ravages of time. A coat of 'rusticles,' created by iron-eating bacteria, covers the remnants of the hull. In time, she will be no more.

"Court rulings have done little to protect the vessel, since she lies in international waters. The many visits by submersibles, landing on the bow, have hastened her demise and eventually another tragedy could result. Even two miles [3 km] down, she is still as vulnerable as ever."

Extract from a speech given by the author.

TIME LINE
1991—1999

1992
Official British Government reappraisal decides that *Californian* could not have been the "mystery ship."

1995
Hollywood director James Cameron shoots footage for his epic movie using Russian submersibles.

1996
A 22-ton (24-tonne) hull section, or the "Big Piece," is almost floated to the surface using giant diesel fuel bags—but breaks away and falls back to the ocean floor.

1998
The sub *Nautile* makes its 100th dive to the wreck, and helps this time to recover the "Big Piece." The piece later goes on exhibition.

Above: David Leibowitz and Kimberley Miller scuba diving. They later married on the bow of the Titanic.

Above: *An underwater photo taken of the Titanic's rusted bow.*

> "On April 15, 1912, the world awoke to the news that the RMS *Titanic* had met with disaster off the coast of Newfoundland. And ever since that time, the misinterpretation of the evidence that was given at the Courts of Inquiry has perpetuated the myth that the *Titanic* collided with an iceberg."

From the book *The Sinking of the Titanic, The Mystery Solved* (2003) by Captain L. M. Collins. Collins suggests that the ship ran on to pack ice that tore its bottom.

hundreds of items, including postcards, paper money, and business cards, using a technique called electrolysis. In 2000, all of the artifacts collected were taken to a laboratory in the United States owned by RMS Titanic, Inc.

SCIENCE OF THE TITANIC

The U.S. company RMS Titanic was finally named salvor-in-possession of the shipwreck in 1994. The company carries out archaeological surveys and scientific analysis, working with the Center for Maritime and Underwater Resource Management (CMURM), experts in underwater archaeology. Microbiologist Roy Cullimore has carried out investigations into the deterioration of the wreck and has discovered that up to 20 percent of the bow of the *Titanic* has already been lost to corrosion. This discovery has led to calls for breaking into the wreck to retrieve items before the hull collapses completely and buries them forever. Scientists estimate that this collapse could happen in less than a century.

RMS Titanic, Inc., has also had forensic engineers examine why the vessel broke in two when it sank. They concluded that stresses in its midsection caused the *Titanic* to bend and eventually buckle during the disaster. Studying the scatter of material on the seabed has also provided clues as to the phases of the ship's breakup. Exciting work using sonar technology has also enabled the RMS Titanic, Inc., to capture images of the damage caused by the iceberg. The pictures taken show that, remarkably, the damage was not one great hole but rather a series of thin slits torn into the boat.

Left: *A robotic arm retrieves a leaded glass window from the Titanic's wreck in 1991.*

Above: *A scientist holds a cherub statue recovered in 1987 from a first-class staircase of the Titanic.*

Below: *A silk bow tie and other personal belongings from a suitcase retrieved from Titanic wreckage.*

2002
Identification of the "Unknown Child" from a bone fragment after the grave was controversially opened in May 2001.

2004
Titanic's foremast, which had been lying against the bridge, collapses into the forward well deck as rust deterioration steadily claims the ship.

2012
The 100th Anniversary of the *Titanic's* voyage. Plans are under way to re-create the exact maiden voyage, in the same places and on the same dates—but without the iceberg.

"A recently advanced theory claims that the *Titanic* was really lost because of a bunker fire. This hypothesis ranges from the implausible (a weakening of the steel from heat) to the incredible (that the iceberg was just a ruse to cover up a darker negligence of incompetent fire-fighting). No evidence is provided—or even a decent explanation of how a fire in a 15-foot-deep [4.5-m-deep] bunker could compromise a hull along a 250-foot [76-m] impact zone. [But] simply mention the word 'cover-up' and all ears are riveted."

Expert Bill Sauder, writing in 1997 in
The Titanic Commutator, **official journal of the U.S.-based Titanic Historical Society, Inc.**

Above: *Divers raising part of the hull to the surface.*

Although the fate of the Titanic was set from the moment it struck ice, the reactions of those on board played a crucial role in determining what would happen next. The crew of the ship acted in a number of different ways—some heroic and some less so. Passengers and crew fortunate enough to survive provided the British and U.S. inquiries into the disaster with valuable accounts of what happened as the ship went down.

EDWARD JOHN SMITH, Captain

Edward John Smith was born on January 27, 1850, in Staffordshire, England. He began studying for a career on the seas in 1871, and he joined the White Star Line in 1880. Just seven years later, Smith was given his first command. During the Boer War in South Africa, Smith commanded several troopships and established a reputation as a skilled sea captain. In 1904, he became commodore of the White Star fleet. Smith often took charge of White Star Line's newest ships on their maiden voyages and the Titanic was no exception. Despite his skills and experience, however, Smith seemed to act in an indecisive way after the Titanic struck the iceberg, and he died on board the ship. His body has never been found. The British Board of Trade cleared Smith of negligence although it believed that the Titanic had been traveling at an "excessive speed." The U.S. Senate, on the other hand, found Smith at fault for the tragedy.

WILLIAM MURDOCH, First Officer

William Murdoch was born on February 28, 1873, in Dalbeattie, Scotland. After serving on various sailing vessels, he joined the White Star Line. Murdoch was the officer on watch who tried to avoid the iceberg. An experienced mariner, he also played a leading role in ensuring a disciplined evacuation for the starboard lifeboats. Murdoch fired shots to clear men out of lifeboats and accounts at the official inquiries testify to his bravery. He died during the tragedy and his body was never found.

CHARLES LIGHTOLLER, Second Officer

Charles Lightoller was born on March 30, 1874, in Lancashire, England. He began his career at sea when he was just 13 years old. He joined the White Star Line in 1900 and quickly moved up the ranks to become Second Officer of the Titanic. Lightoller helped rescue many passengers during the the sinking and was the most senior surviving officer. In 1940, at the age of 60, Lightoller commanded the Sundowner in a dangerous mission to rescue soldiers from the beaches at Dunkirk during World War II. He died on December 8, 1952, six years after retiring from the British navy.

HERBERT JOHN PITMAN, Third Officer

Herbert John Pitman was born on November 20, 1877, in Somerset, England. At the age of eighteen, he joined the Merchant Navy and went on to qualify as a master mariner. In 1906, he joined the White Star Line. He was on board the *Titanic* for her sea trials as well as for the maiden voyage. Pitman's duties included determining the ship's position, supervising the deck, and standing watch on the bridge. At the hearings in the United States and Great Britain, Pitman reported that there were no lifeboat drills. During the disaster, Pitman helped with the uncovering and launching of several of the lifeboats and escaped himself to the safety of the *Carpathia*. Pitman later served on the *Titanic's* sister ship, the *Olympic*, and also served in World War II. Pitman died on December 7, 1961.

J. BRUCE ISMAY, Managing Director of the White Star Line

J. (Joseph) Bruce Ismay was born on December 2, 1862, near Liverpool, England. He was the son of a founder of the White Star Line. Ismay took charge of the firm when his father died in 1899. In 1901, he began the negotiations that resulted in the company becoming part of the International Mercantile Marine (IMM), a U.S. firm. Ismay regularly boarded the maiden voyages of his ships and was on board as a first-class passenger for the Titanic's first (and last) trip. Ismay left in one of the last boats and was heavily criticized by the press for saving himself while so many of his passengers died. Ismay retired the year after the sinking, unable to carry on in the face of such criticism. He lived quietly, often at his Irish fishing retreat, until his death in 1937.

ARCHIBALD GRACIE, U.S. Passenger

Colonel Archibald Gracie was born on January 17, 1859, in Alabama. He graduated from West Point and eventually became a colonel in the United States Army. He was a member of the wealthy Gracie family but also became wealthy in his own right through a real estate business. Gracie boarded the *Titanic* at Southampton as a first-class passenger and was one of those who survived by climbing on top of the overturned Collapsible B. He tried to revive a fellow passenger before being rescued by the *Carpathia*. He went on to write a book, *The Truth about the Titanic,* but he never fully recovered his good health after the *Titanic*'s sinking. He died on December 4, 1912, before he had finished proofing his book and before it was published. Many of the *Titanic's* survivors attended Gracie's funeral.

LAWRENCE BEESLEY, British Passenger

Second-class passenger Lawrence Beesley was born on December 31, 1877, in Derbyshire, England. An avid scholar and Cambridge graduate, Beesley became a science instructor at Dulwich College, England, in 1904. Beesley boarded the *Titanic* at Southampton as a second-class passenger. Saved in "lucky" lifeboat 13, Beesley and his fellow occupants endured a moment of terror when it seemed lifeboat 15 would fall on top of them as it was lowered from the *Titanic*'s deck. After his dramatic rescue, Beesley, like other survivors, was inspired to write a book about the disaster and wrote *The Loss of the SS Titanic*. He also attended the filming of the movie *A Night to Remember* and actually attempted to stay on board the ship as the sinking scenes were filmed. Beesley died on February 14, 1967, at age 89.

COLONEL JOHN JACOB ASTOR, U.S. Passenger

Colonel John Jacob Astor IV was born in New York on July 13, 1864. Educated at Harvard, he was an inventor, writer, and businessman. In the 1890s, Astor built some of New York's finest hotels, including the Waldorf-Astoria. During the Spanish-American War, he became a lieutenant colonel in the U.S. Volunteers. Astor married for the first time in 1891 but created a stir in 1909 when he divorced his wife to marry eighteen-year-old Madeleine Force. After spending time abroad to escape gossip, Astor and his new wife decided to return to the United States in the spring of 1912 on the *Titanic*. When the ship struck ice, Astor remained unconcerned and was reluctant to leave the ship. He stayed on board while his wife was loaded into a lifeboat, and he lost his life in the disaster. Madeleine Astor died on March 27, 1940.

SENATOR WILLIAM ALDEN SMITH, Chairman, U.S. Senate Inquiry

William Alden Smith was born on May 12, 1859, in Michigan. He began his career practicing law and served as a U.S. Senator from 1907 to 1919. Smith was not knowledgeable in maritime matters, but he persuaded U.S. president William Howard Taft to allow him to hold an inquiry into the *Titanic* disaster as soon as the survivors landed. Officers and crew, including the White Star Line's managing director J. Bruce Ismay, were served with subpoenas when they arrived. Smith's inquiry yielded much interesting information, despite his occasional apparent ignorance (he reportedly once asked what an iceberg was made of). Smith was very interested in finding out the name of the mystery ship seen when the *Titanic* was sinking. The U.S. inquiry infuriated the British, who regarded their ship as none of America's business.

ARTHUR ROSTRON, *Carpathia* Captain

Arthur Rostron was born on May 14, 1869, in Lancashire, England. At the age of just thirteen he joined a Merchant Navy training ship and set out to sea. Rostron went on to join the Cunard Line in 1895 and commanded many of the line's great ships. He briefly left the line to serve in the British navy during the Russo-Japanese War. On April 11, 1912, he guided the *Carpathia* out of New York toward Europe. It was on this journey that the ship would come to the aid of the *Titanic*. Rostron won the U.S. Congressional Gold Medal for his role in rescuing the *Titanic's* passengers. Rostron, however, preferred to praise his crew and wireless operator, who reportedly caught the distress message while unlacing his boots just before going to bed. Rostron died on November 4, 1940.

ROBERT HICHENS, *Titanic* Quartermaster

Robert Hichens was born on September 16, 1882, in Cornwall, England. By 1906, he had reached the level of master mariner and had served on many different vessels. He was at the wheel when the *Titanic* struck an iceberg, and he was later put in charge of lifeboat 6, which contained only women. Without a crew, the women were forced to row. Several women later complained about his coarseness and said he voiced doubts that they could survive. They also reported that he ignored requests to row back to collect more passengers. The matter was raised at both the U.S. and British inquiries. Hichens went on to serve on other ships, but in 1933, he shot a man over a debt and was sent to jail. He was released in 1937, and he died on September 23, 1940, aboard the cargo ship *English Trader* during World War II.

LORD MERSEY, British Inquiry President

John Charles Bigham was born on August 3, 1840, in Liverpool, England. He worked as a barrister and judge, and when he retired in 1910, he was made Lord Mersey. Lord Mersey was chosen by the British government to chair the investigation into the heavy loss of life on the *Titanic*. Mersey presided over the British inquiry—which Officer Lightoller later described as a "whitewash" since it cleared the British Board of Trade, responsible for shipping regulations, of any wrongdoing. Lord Mersey turned in a report that concluded that the accident could not have been anticipated. His obituary in the *London Times* in 1929 noted that "he was exceedingly quick and clever, but he was too apt to take short cuts; and he was by no means free from the judicial fault of premature expression of opinion or bias."

astern toward the rear, or stern, of a ship.

berth (v) to bring a ship to dock or moorings; (n) a place for a ship to tie up.

bow often expressed in plural (bows), the leading knife-edge or forward part of a ship.

bridge the control room of a ship.

bulkheads metal walls that create compartments and are designed to retain water, fire, or gas.

capsized turned over.

commissioned ordered; formally assigned a certain task or function.

compartments contained areas within a larger structure.

complacency a feeling of calm pleasure or a sense of self-satisfaction or security, particularly when unaware of or in spite of possible dangers.

CQD "Come Quick Danger" or "all stations-danger;" an early maritime distress signal that was later replaced by SOS, a signal more easily transmitted via Morse code in telegraphy.

debris remains or fragments of something broken or destroyed.

disembark leave a ship.

DNA deoxyribonucleic acid, a double-stranded molecule that carries genes along its strands. Since the genetic material DNA carries is unique to each human, scientists can use it to discover the identity of human remains.

emigrant a person who leaves his or her home country to permanently settle in another country.

forecastle the forward part of a ship, usually crew quarters.

freighter a ship that carries only or mostly cargo.

funnel a tube or shaft that allows smoke or steam to escape, especially on a ship.

gantry a framelike structure or bridge, usually having one or more traveling cranes that run on tracks, used in the construction of ships.

growlers low-lying, small icebergs.

home rule the granting of governing powers by a central government to a local or regional government. In 1912, Great Britain's parliament was considering a bill that would give Ireland, then under its control, a greater amount of home rule.

hull the outer plating or lower frame of a ship.

inchoate incomplete; just begun; not fully developed.

infer to assume, speculate, or guess a conclusion based on given information.

jeopardize endanger or put at risk.

keel a structural part of a ship that extends along the center of the ship's bottom from its bows to its stern.

knot a unit of measurement equal to one nautical mile (approximately 1.15 miles or 1.85 km) per hour, used to measure a ship's speed or the speed of an aircraft.

latitude the angular distance from Earth's North or South Poles, expressed in degrees.

longitude the angular distance measured east or west along the arc, or curve, of Earth using imaginary lines, called meridians, that extend from the North to the South Pole. The measurement is expressed in degrees.

memoir personal written recollections; an autobiography.

moorings ropes or chains that hold a ship secure in its berth.

Morse code a code devised by Samuel Morse that uses a pattern of dots and dashes to represent letters of the alphabet. Morse code is used in sending telegraphs or in sending messages through the flashing of lights.

navigation the act of plotting or determining a ship's course or position; the act of traveling on, over, or through water.

obituary newspaper article announcing a person's death and usually including a brief biography.

onerous burdensome.

port (1) a city or town along a coast where ships load and unload or take shelter from a storm; (2) the left side of a ship.

promenade deck a deck for walking or strolling.

rivets metal bolts or pins used to hold two pieces of material together. A rivet has a head on one end. Another head is beaten into the other end once the rivet is passed through a hole in each of the pieces. The two heads keep the pieces in place.

rusticles a name given to formations of rust that look like icicles.

salvage saving or rescuing a ship or its cargo from destruction or danger.

shuffleboard a game in which players take turns using sticks, or cues, to push a disk toward numbered areas marked on the floor. The number in the area where the disk stops determines the player's score.

sidelight a light on the side of a ship. A ship has a green light on its starboard side and a red light on its port side. At night or in fog, the different colors help other ships determine what side of a ship is visible.

Solent the channel or body of water that lies between England and the Isle of Wight.

sonar describing a method used for detecting underwater objects through first transmitting soundwaves, and then measuring the time it takes for an echo to return and the direction from which it returns, to determine the object's distance and dimensions.

SOS an international distress message popularly believed to stand for "Save Our Souls" or "Save Our Ship." The letters SOS were actually chosen because of the ease in which they could be transmitted via Morse code.

starboard the right side of a ship.

stateroom passenger cabin.

steerage the accommodations on a ship for passengers who are paying the lowest fares.

stern the rear part of a ship.

stokehold the space in a ship that houses the ship's boilers or the spaces in front of the boilers from which the furnaces are fed; fireroom.

submersible a small submarine used to carry out underwater research at very great depths.

subpoena a legal notice to appear in court or submit certain objects or documents as evidence in a trial. A person who does not comply with a subpoena faces legal penalties.

superstructure the structure above the deck on a ship; deck buildings.

tarpaulins heavy waterproof coverings.

tenders ships employed to attend to a larger ship, supplying the larger ship with provisions or ferrying its passengers to and from a dock.

thwarts planks laid across a small boat and used for seating.

Turkish bath a bath in which the bather spends time in a series of steam rooms, each increasing in temperature, before he or she takes a cold shower and, finally, receives a massage.

weigh in shipping, to raise the anchor.

well deck a sunken deck located between a ship's superstructures.

wireless telegraphy the process of sending an electronic message in Morse code by radio waves.

Please visit our web site at: **www.garethstevens.com**
**For a free color catalog describing Gareth Stevens Publishing's
list of high-quality books and multimedia programs,
call 1-800-542-2595 or 1-800-387-3178 (Canada).
Gareth Stevens Publishing's fax: (414) 332-3567.**

Library of Congress Cataloging-in-Publication Data

Molony, Senan, 1963–
    Titanic: a primary source history / Senan Molony.
      p. cm. — (In their own words)
    Includes bibliographical references and index.
    ISBN 0-8368-5980-4 (lib. bdg.)
    1. Titanic (Steamship)—Juvenile literature. 2. Shipwrecks—North Atlantic
Ocean—Juvenile literature. 3. Titanic (Steamship)—Sources—Juvenile
literature. 4. Shipwrecks—North Atlantic Ocean—Sources—Juvenile literature.
I. Title. II. In their own words (Milwaukee, Wis.)
    G530.T6M626   2005
    910'.9163'4—dc22   2005040897

This North American edition first published in 2006 by
Gareth Stevens Publishing
A Member of the WRC Media Family of Companies
330 West Olive Street, Suite 100
Milwaukee, WI 53212 USA

This U.S. edition copyright © 2006 by Gareth Stevens, Inc.
Original edition copyright © 2005 ticktock Entertainment Ltd.
First published in Great Britain in 2005 by ticktock Media Ltd.,
Unit 2, Orchard Business Centre, North Farm Road,
Tunbridge Wells, Kent, TN2 3XF, U.K.

Gareth Stevens editor: Monica Rausch
Gareth Stevens art direction: Tammy West
Gareth Stevens designer: Jenni Gaylord

Photo credits: (b=bottom; c=center; l=left; r=right; t=top)
Alamy: 4-5(c), 10(b), 18(t), 24(t). CORBIS: 1, 9(b), 14–15(c), 21(t), 28(b),
29(t), 35(t), 36(b), 37(t), 37(b), 38-30(all). Everett Collection: 2, 7(b),
23(t), 32-33(c), 33(t). Getty Images: 8(l), 13(b), 30(c). National Maritime
Museum: 6(b), 10(c), 14(cl), 18(b), 21(tc), 22(all), 23(b), 25(c). Senan
Molony: 16(b), 20(b), 24(cl), 29(b), 30(tl), 31(t), 34(t), 36(tl), 40-43(all).

Printed in the United States of America

1 2 3 4 5 6 7 8 9 09 08 07 06 05